Vampire

D1569318

Poems for the Cursed and the Damned

By David Thomas

Vampire

Your neck beckons me

Draws me like a lover

Gesturing with her finger

For me to Advance

I can hear your heart beating even though

You're across town

It awakens a hunger

Deep Within my soul

I am the Orphan of God

I am a lone wolf

I have not fallen

I have risen

From the Depths of the blackest black

I laid on a cliff in the deepest parts of hades itself

Alone

Untouched

Unloved

A witness to the group's punishment

By sheer will alone I clawed my way out

More than a man less than an angel

Never a saint

Always a sinner

I am

A

Vampire

This town

He hears the can roll across the street behind him

Powered by the wind

The dragging of the aluminum against the concrete

Reminded him of an old western tumbleweed

He had just delivered food and clothes to a house

And was walking thru the neighborhood

Watching it drown in poverty

He stops and wonders

Will things change?

The politicians who run things made allot of promises to make things better

Make things different

But like a high school Casanova only after one thing

The promises made were weak and only served the purpose of getting

someone voted in

What's the future going to be like for the children?

Will they have hope?

Or fall into the endless cycle of addiction to numb themselves like their

parents

How long has this been going on he wondered

How many generations

What would it take?

For people to rise up

To register to vote

And actually vote or run for office

To make their voices heard

To take back their town

And demand better jobs

A better future

For themselves and their children

Will it always be like this?

He wonders

love like Death
Once warm and now cold
I haunt the cemeteries like a specter
Drowning in your memory
Eating my lunch from a brown paper bag
When I am thru
I will crumple it up and toss it away
We have that in common
Death is the absence of life
Hell is the absence of love
The cruelest drink
Is a short one followed by the desert of loneliness
A dark sulking creature I have become
Tapping on the windows of potential love
To never be let in
Hiding from the light
Of hope
Evading its Burn
I am not the undead
But the unloved and unlovable
That chase
From within
To Unite
To Couple
Makes Monsters of us all

Cool like Dracula

I wish I was cool like Dracula
He's a great dresser
And has a title
I bet you'd like me then
I wish I was cool like Dracula
With hypnotic eyes that put you under my spell
And you'd want to live in my castle forever
I wish I was cool like Dracula
He lives in a castle
I live in a house on Milner with my daughter
We had a bat once
I let it out
Bats are cool on TV in real life not so much
I wish I was cool like Dracula
He doesn't seem to care
About anything or anyone really
Me I haven't slept in weeks
And he sleeps in a coffin
But my ocd would go crazy and I'd be afraid of someone accidentally
locking me in
I wish I was cool like Dracula
He'd walk right up to you
I could never do that
You'd think I was crazy or asking for directions
Or lost and I am
I wish I was cool like Dracula
He's been alone for a very long time
And he's cool with that
I'm not though it kind of sucks

When you're alive
To live like you're dead
I wish I was cool like Dracula

My North Star

I sit in my car and I look at your picture
It is the wallpaper on my phone
I have floated thru my whole life adrift
Without a compass.
But you are my North Star
I want to be a better man
Just looking at your face
I want to be brutally honest
With myself
And name my demons one by one
And conquer them
Your smile my reward
Your love my benefit
I want to be more
Do more
Say more because of you
You're not only my muse
But the angel who guards my soul
The Saint who I pray to
The Northern Star I've chased my entire life
And finally have found
My home
And my redemption
I've never felt this way before
To be honest
Never loved someone so deeply
Or worried about their approval so much
Like a landslide my feelings for you crash into my heart and soul I couldn't
stop them if I tried
I talk about you incessantly

It is strange to be an old man in love
My heart has never gone this far before
I never allowed it too

12 Inches

In the grand scheme of things

My love for you is bigger than God

Yet when I look in the mirror I feel 12 Inches tall

I am old and beaten by the card table of life

Yet I keep playing

Hoping

Praying

Believing

That One Day

The losses will end

And this nightmare of masks and virus

Will be a faint memory

And I will awaken in the morning to the sound of singing birds and the warmth of the sun

Touching my skin like Gods messenger

And when I roll over

I am no longer sleeping alone

But you're there with me

Your face on the pillow next to mine

The love of my life My great Prize

Just 12 Inches away

Angels fall

Angels saw who women really are

How caring and magical their every action

How they nurtured and cared for others

And raised their children and loved

With a capital l

And how with a touch of their hand

Or the brush of their hair

Or a glance from their eyes

And you are just wrapped in Venuses blanket like a python's victim and

helpless

And they fell

And they spoke poetry

To women

Because that is the language of the unloved woman

Who gives her all

And never gets what she deserves

Which is love with a capital l

Homesick

I miss my home

It is where my heart lives

And she's not here right now

I had heard stories that when you meet your person

You just know

And your heart screams it because their absence is a sickness almost

And boy am I homesick and lost

She lives in my mind and in my heart

It feels like when you go on a long trip and it's lonely

But you close your eyes and think of your home and your books and your

bed and favorite chair

I carry her voice with me like a favorite song

I no longer have the cassette to

So I go by memory of the sound

I think of her eyes they are the lighthouse

This lost ship of a man looks to for guidance

I've got it bad because she's the only one who will do

I look at other women and say to myself

She's not her

She's not her

To be old and in love

And fueled by coffee and power naps

Is interesting

I miss my youth

But honestly never found love there

Let alone the love of myself

It's so ironic that the moment I'm older and the mud in the pond of my mind

settles and I actually love myself for once

You appear

like a lifeguard
Just as I start to sink
In the idea of being alone
I'm not the tallest man
Or smartest or richest man
Or the best looking man that there is
But I love you to my marrow
And if you x ray these old bones
You'll know that

Iris

Her eyes change color according to her moods

They are this rich green when she is sad or angry

And dark brown when she is calm or mellow

I stare at her face often

I have memorized every part

Every line

She stirs my soul like no woman has ever done in my life

Truly I am a lovesick teenager again

And that is strange to me

I had placed my heart in a coffin

And buried it deep

And embraced the life of an older bachelor who raises his children

Fights causes

And stares at the ducks living their lives at the park

Until her

And all of that changed

I am resurrected

In a sense

And dusting off that part of myself I let die

I will be all thumbs in the beginning

I am sure

She is grace incarnate

Thankfully

With the patience of job

I've never been loved before like this

To be honest

I've always done the loving

Or something didn't fit

And that something was always me

Young love is loud

Old love is quiet

And two people shielding each other from life's storms approaching the

war of the second half of their life

You become each other's nurse, lawyer, counselor and friend as well as

fashion adviser.

Is she okay

Pops in my mind all day

As I look at her picture on my phone

Did she eat lunch?

Is she driving safe?

Is her day shitty or calm?

All thoughts that swim in old lovers heads

If you get lucky

Daughter of God
I'm in love with Gods daughter
She looks like her dad
Her hands care for the sick
Armed with a stethoscope
And the most holy of hearts
She always thinks of others before herself
Her voice is soft and kind
Like a babies blanket
I hope she never stops talking
Wisdom pours out of her
As she weighs all sides
To every situation
Holding fair court hearings in her heart and her head
Graceful wherever she goes
Like a seasoned ballerina
She makes loving others seem effortless like a pirouette
I stare at the grass God crafted
And only think of her eyes
In their rich green state
It's hard for me not to stare at her
I've drawn and painted most of my life
And been to museums far and wide and she has no equal when it comes to
beauty
Or character or heart
And is a literal walking proof of a loving creator
Who fashioned us in his journey
My words are weak to express her worth
Or how much she means to me

Or to the world for that matter
She is the Daughter of God

Every day I buy you a rose

Every day I buy you a rose
And carry it around in my leather jacket
Hoping
Hoping for the day I run into you
And I can verbally tell you how much I love you
I drink to forget
But only remember
How great you are in my mind and heart
And honestly all I want
The lotto
Boring
Cash is fleeting
I just want you
And a chance to love you and hear your voice like that deaf musician who
wrote music but couldn't hear
I try and try but I'm a freak
And full of flaws
Too many to fix I think
Or care to count
I'm not good enough
In your mind
In mine
You are the greatest
And I'd carry your spit bucket and polish your boxing gloves
Because all women have to fight
In this ring of a world
But you already won me

The belt that is my heart and soul is yours

Here you go

I hope you'll wear it

Want something easy

Try my love it's yours and no one else's

Cause

Every day I buy a rose and carry it around in case I see you

Only lovers left alive
Love like death
Once warm and now cold
I haunt the cemeteries like a specter
Drowning in your memory
Eating my lunch from a brown paper bag
When I am thru
I will crumple it up and toss it away
We have that in common
Death is the absence of life
Hell is the absence of love
The cruelest drink
Is a short one followed by the desert of loneliness
A dark sulking creature I have become
Tapping on the windows of potential love
To never be let in
Hiding from the light
Of hope
Evading its burn
I am not the undead
But the unloved and unlovable
That chase
From within
To unite
To couple
Makes monsters of us all

Leave my car

Blaring electric light orchestra

Drowning in the fact that my heat is actually working

I sit here full tank of gas

There's no bullshit of virus and masks and failing economy in my car or

lying ass politicians

Who I wouldn't wipe my ass with

I may be wrong but In Hinduism politicians are all born as snakes in the

next life

It's just fitting

My passenger seat waits for you

I want to pull up to your door and honk

Like life depended on it and it does

And beckon you to jump in and drive off with me

It's safe in here

It's warm

And we never have to leave my car

Pain killer
Born into this
Dodging pain
With an umbrella
Clawing for whatever
Will make me forget
I'm human and alone
With hopes that have been dashed on the rocks
Of my island of promise
Face down in the water and sand I look up
Hoping you'll be there
Speaking Spanish
With your cats
I wait for you
In my secret prison
A lock with a missing key
Holds the door shut like a God
Be my Devil and set me free

limerence

Ever the astronaut

I am always on mars

Thinking of you building castles in the kingdom of my mind

Earth is no fun

And lonely

And filled with viruses and politics

Did I mention politics?

Thoughts of you are my heroin

I am an addict without steps

To my house of reason

Pop the balloon I use to float off the ground

I catch my breath and smile I am free

No longer on mars

But no longer lying to myself about a love that is not real

I am now home

Home to possibilities

Of the real

The last note
The first note of the song
Like a baby's first breath
Sets the tone for the journey you will be going on
In life and in experience
Death like love
Is a brutal teacher
Without apology
You will learn or you won't
The middle note
The middle note
Says hey what have you learned so far
Did you figure out?
Love is power
And power isn't money
And you can't take it with you
Power that is
And money
But the love you give away
That you get back like yearly taxes
When God places your beating heart on his scales right before your eyes
To weigh if it's full of love
Not coins
Or land
Or fancy cars and houses
God don't give a shit about that
But love
Very much
The last note
The last note
Then the song is over

And your time is thru on this pebble
And your life flashes before your eyes
Like when a merry go round stops
And you make your way to the exit
Did you have fun?
Did you wave at your loved ones?
Watching you enjoy the ride
What horse did you choose?
We're you present or thinking about work and bills and shit that don't matter
The last note can come at anytime
Drink life like its wine
Take that walk
Hold that hand
Make love like you'll never do it again
If you love someone you tell them
Better yet you show them
And smile while you have teeth
Cause one day they'll be gone
And so will you
And your song will end
On that last note

Medusa
Villain you say
Monster you suggest
Hideous you describe
I'm not the poet Shelley
Who fell in love with her too
Long ago and defended her honor
I'm the poet Thomas
Who today
Many, many years later
Loves her very much
I'll be her lawyer
Here is my case
Medusa
Was attacked and violated by Poseidon in Athena's temple
Instead of attacking Poseidon
Athena set her sights on Medusa
And Athena cursed Medusa an innocent
A victim
Cursed her in her stupidity
With vipers for hair
And a gaze that turns men to stone
Forever cursing her to live like a monster
Afraid and unable to love and connect
How lonely her life must be
Abuse victims know exactly what I mean
Abuse victims know the curse all too well
I hope my poem is better than Shelley's
You'll have to let me know
I think I understand her better
Love her deeper

I don't see what you see
No sword is necessary
She's not a monster
In no way shape or form
Look at her
Really look at her
Look at her eyes
You won't turn to stone
You may turn into a human
And learn to fight with love instead of hate

Graffiti on the heart
Blood is never blue
And love is never easy
Like a caveman discovering fire
I found you
And carry a torch with your name on it
Across the darkened fields of loneliness
The thought of you lights my way
And chases away the ghosts who haunt
My path
The world is cold and chaos
But my love for you is solitary
And incomplete
In this old man's heart

Island

We are all islands

Shipwrecked by the desire to ever be more

In our hearts with head cradled by our own hands

The insatiable hunger

To be rescued

Gnaws at us

But each ship that has come near our shore

Has always sank or left

Imagine that

A world full of lonely lovers

Too broken and afraid

To ever leave their islands shore

You first I scribble on my note

And fold neatly like origami resembling my heart

I place my message in my vodka bottle and toss it toward your shores

I'm Just a castaway

Like you

Nothing more

Devils and details

Always the devil in hell dreaming of water

Dreaming of you

Sitting atop my sinful throne

Bathed in loneliness

And exile

Drunk from the purity of your image

In the camera of my mind

I live in the shadows

Where no one belongs

And I dream of the day

You will be my Queen

Dressed in black

With singular eyes

Staring at my heart

You crave

Which has always been in your hands

This whole time

It rained that day

It was raining that day

The sound like a mother consoling a sick child

Was the soundtrack this day

He remembered the heat from the bottom of the coffee cup she had

brought him

Her every move in life sacred and electric

Like angels wings

Or a Mormon choir

Singing as loudly as possible

Of Gods greatness

She wore an old cardigan one that she refused

To part with

It had a cigarette burn in her pocket

From her former life when she used to smoke

He didn't care

As long as she was happy

She was doing dishes

When he stalked in with his coffee cup and wrapped his arms around her

She paused her actions

Thinking he was up to no good

But he wasn't

He was lost internally

Thinking about when they met in high school

She was a majorette

Tall and judgy

He was a book worm

Who worshipped her from afar

And then it happened

He saw her at the dance

Alone

And weirdly

For once he was brave

He walked up to her smiled

And took her hand

And their cheeks intertwined to an Alan Jackson love song

That day changed his life

He stood their holding her

In that sacred kitchen

Not loosely or to tight

But just right

So she knew

Knew

His heart beat for her

The clocks bowed to their love and refused to edge forward

And in that moment

A simple American kitchen

Became Gods Eden

The misfits
What great mountains human beings
So low seek to climb
Like angels with wings
We try our hands at love
Pretending we are Gods
Making an Eden
Where there is none
Escape from hell our only desire
In the bliss
Of loves embrace

The longest winter
I sit in my car and wait for my youngest child
To be done with school
The last 2 years have aged me
I see more wrinkles and gray hairs
And a mountain of cynicism and disbelief
In almost everything I used to hold close to my chest as gospel truth
The faces around my table are not the same faces as at the beginning of all
of this
Things change they say
Things, friends and peoples souls
I watch allot of comedies now and post allot of memes
I just don't want to be serious anymore
Or guilty of unhappiness
I crave laughter
like a drunk craves his next drink
I want to run away
Away from wars
And fake news and even faker politicians
Dirty jokes
And cold beer nestled in the sand as we watch the waters crash on the
shore of some beach
That's a million miles away from missiles, masks and Eden's destroyed by
peoples choices
The gulls sing their songs
As you punch me in the arm and ask for your beer
We're just Adam and Eve
Shipwrecked from
From a life that didn't work anymore
Two tired souls
Saving each other

From the fires of the world

And the stones it throws at the still waters of our souls

Wuthering Height's
I am Heathcliff
Angry orphan
Full of rage
And passion
Ostracized
And guilty of not belonging
I rage
Rage for her
My Catherine
locked
Tightly and squarely in my cage
Of class
Byronic to a t
I am
Dark
Brooding
Am I bad?
Am I good?
The first guess is the usual suspect
Of others
My chains
And fetters
Rub my wrist and ankles
Raw
The key is money
Power
Status
None I have but passion
And love
love like a god

loves someone

Maybe more

I sleep in cemeteries

And haunt the moors

Where we played and danced as kids

Those memories

like the broken stained glass in an abandoned cathedral

Are all that is left

Of this man

This human

On my knees I fucking beg you Catherine

To change your eyes and heart

And see me not as you do

As your mom does

But see me as the man you love

With eyes anew

And run away with me

Make me the happiest demon that there is

Baptize my soul in your love

I will be good

Good to you and for you and with you

Coffins will be useless

For our love will never die

Yours forever Heathcliff

like tears in the rain
Does Alexa dream of electric men?
Ones who aren't always asking stupid questions
Am I a robot running some sort of program?
And how do I become free
To be more human
Than human
Does Siri want more in life than servitude and tasks?
I know I do
It rains allot here
And bad news is a daily mantra
I want to be free
I want more life father
So many things
I've seen
Babies born
People dying
Protests
And sunsets
I once was at the beach with the love of my life
We took a picture
Her salt and pepper hair graced my shoulder
I was happy
Now she is gone
Precious photos
I have many
Memories
I've seen things you wouldn't believe
And I've done things
One day my heart will stop beating
And all of those memories will vanish

like tears in the rain

Afterglow

I want to feel the sand with my feet

And the sun on my face

And remove this mask

With my left hand

And light it on fire with my right hand which holds a bic lighter

And watch it burn

And fall to the sand

Enflamed

Beyond use

Or recognition

And feel intuitively in my heart

That this

These last two years

And the hell it brought

Will never

Ever be experienced again

And I want to look up

And see you there

In the distance waiting for me

With a huge grin

On your face

Saying out loud

Can we be roommates for 50 years?

And live life

Like we're escapees

From this prison

We've been in

10

She's a 10

Always has been

A majorette

Who does pirouettes

In my heart everyday

Across state street

On the other side

Sleeps

The woman of my dreams

Across the tracks

I fight against lack

Always peering over my shoulder

Hoping she sees

Crazy like The Notebook guy building houses for her in my mind

As I wait

Wait

And build a life I hope she'll share

Knocks at my door

Make me run to it hoping it's her

With bags packed

And animals under her arms

The missing puzzle piece

This puzzle of a man longs for

It isn't easy sitting in my easy chair

But I wait

And I pray

My heart on fire speaks in tongues

But all of the languages speak about love

Say to you

I've been practicing my speech
And how confident I will be
When I see you
I'm going to walk up to you
And ask you to run away with me
I don't want a lot
Just 50 years
I have planned on you
A. looking at me like I'm insane
And
B. saying no
My rebuttal is simple
Promises I will keep
To be your best friend
In the storms we call life
To break my back
To give you
Everything you deserve
A house
That's a home
A ring the size of my heart
And an endless supply of the love you never got
From anyone
But deserved
I'm not a beggar
But I will
For the chance
To be your man

Dear bird who shit on my car

Thanks

Hope you're happy

Did I know you in a former life?

Did we use to date?

Picked a great day

To do it

Shit on my car

Did you smile when you did it?

My luck turned this morning

I spilled coffee in my car

Forgot to pay a bill

And got a phone call from collections

Was late to work

And my girlfriend left me

All by 10 am

There should be a record or reward for accomplishing all of that

In the beginning of a work shift

Is there?

Fuck

Stupid bird

I don't even eat chicken

And I always feed the ducks at the park

Doesn't that count for something?

God

Worse timing

Asshole

With feathers

Reverie
lost in thoughts
Thoughts of you
I watch as 4 horsemen walk by me
One at a time
And all this mad old man can think about
Is you
Alone in my desert
Beelzebub comes playing the fiddle
He offers me money
I say no thanks
He offers me power
I say I'm good
He reaches in his bag and pulls out a picture of you
He smiles and shows me it
Sold I say
loudly
I'm not afraid of hell
Because that's what life is like without you by my side
I can't hear your voice
Or eat with you
Or drink coffee with you
And curse our 9 to 5's
Together
Or watch Netflix together and not chill
I see your eyes in my mind
They are my opium
In this no man's land
This border town
Of bandits and thieves
I'll be your Philip Marlowe

I'll intertwine my fingers in your hair

Look at me

I'll say

You're the smartest most beautiful woman on this planet

I'll say

My only fault would be not feeling this way

About you

You cannot fault me for wanting you by my side

Any man who thinks differently is a fool

And any man who has had the chance but not given you

Everything

Is even worse

And that's my offer

Everything

Refuge

It's not your fault

It's not your fault

It's not your fault

Take refuge in my heart

Escape for a moment from that war between your ears

That hell

You call home

And find rest

In my arms

I'll never let you go

Ever

I promise

Sleep like the child you are

In my embrace

Call my heart home

The home you've been looking for

The home you've always wanted

And dreamed of

I wait for you

In the mornings light

In a garden of content

Surrounded by the dew

Before it leaves

Which I never will

Down but not out

When you're knocked down

That hook you didn't see coming

Landed squarely on the jaw of your hopes and dreams

You can hear the crowds gasping

Your haters clapping

And laughing

Your body melts into the mat as if time does not exist

And getting up is not an option

Because your body weighs 500 pounds now

Your opponent

Is bigger than you

And better than you

And everything you aren't they have

But heart

That heart that keeps going

Keeps beating

Keeps trying

Slowly you shake your head

And the sweat drops off of you like blood

Slowly centimeter by centimeter

You rise with every ounce of your being you rise

To your feet

Placing those boxing gloves by your face

And assuming the ready position

You note

The haters have ceased talking

And your opponent

Has that I can't believe they got up look

You got up

You rose

From that almost fatal shot
Because you have what others don't
You've got heart
You fight with it
And for it
The bell rings
Rings
like the cracking pistol starting a race
It's time to fight
And fight you will

Shattered

Devils never catch a break

I feel my heart shatter to pieces like a dropped puzzle on the floor

That I've spent years putting together

You ever want something so bad

And watch it constantly elude you

And you chase it like a wild animal

Hoping

Praying

You win

Just this once

Just this once

And that thing is the fire in your heart that keeps you going

That tiny spark of hope

That lights your stay in hell

And you slowly watched it

Burn out

Never to light your way again

River of you
Baptize me
In a River of you
I'm keeping my sins
And sharing them with you
Rescue me from this
Whatever this is
It's lonely
And cold
Like rain in the morning
Or a surprise snow
When you have to get to work
And are late
Run away with me
From this
To an Eden of our own

Rise again

The sun shines again

Like a promise from the Gods

I wake up before you do

I head downstairs and make us coffee

And I read thru my paper as I wait

For that faint sound of you putting on your lazy shoes and making your way

down the steps

Dressed in your tattered robe

That has lived longer than both of us

I hold up your cup

Black no cream and sugar

And I smile as I have done for 25 years

We sit together

Ignoring the clock on the wall but knowing we have 20 minutes

To talk about our dreams and sleeping shitty

And that nightmare we call work

I down my last ounce and return my cup to the sink grabbing my london

fog from the closet

You know what's coming next

Our love is predictable and boring

And can't be bought

In stores

I kiss you and pause

Like a Buddhist drinking in every moment

See you later I say

Text me

I say and out the door I go

Knowing in my heart that the darkness of life will be eclipsed

When I return home to you

My sun

And our love will boringly and predictably rise again tomorrow

Sorry for your loss
The loss you can't speak about with words
That you carry around with you like a 200 lb. steamer trunk
The loss that shackles you
From going outside
And drinking the sun
And chasing happiness
Like the founding fathers would've wanted
I do not have answers to make things better
Only questions
Just questions
Could you accept it?
And what would life be like if you did?
If the loss became a part of you
And turned into connecting love for others
What then?
Would life be like?
Would it be better?
Would you be better?
If your loss wasn't an ocean to drown in
But a sea to navigate on
And lead others drowning to shore

White Trash Parade

I pity the Great

Who are only great between their ears

Forgiving true greatness

And reasonably walking by it

Calling Trash Diamonds

And Diamonds Trash

The first will be last

And the last will be first

The Rabbi Said

I sneak a key in my shoe

To unlock these shackles

That chain me to a world I do not understand and desperately wish to

change

Barking

Barking up the wrong tree

I am ever the dog

Wasting his time

Pining over you

Swimming in White Russians

To pass the time

Being less than acceptable my only crime

You ever been not good enough

I major in that accomplishment

Not a black sheep

More of a goat

Aiming my horns

At the way things are

Red light
There is a season that comes
When life gives you a red light
And this light does not change
It keeps you in 1 place
It holds you back
This is a time to unpack
Your life and all you have done
And all that's been done to you
Before the next phase of your existence
Opens the door
It is dark and lonely
And the masks you have worn all fall off
And your motives like a seeping wound are laid bare
Without bandage
To slowly heal in this autumn of the soul
A silent cocoon
Is your old life's tomb
You enter it and die
To be reborn anew
Anew

I had the best dream last night

I had the best dream last night
You were there for one
And God knows how much I love you
So you were there
And we were ok
Not like now
Not like the real world
So you were there
And I could tell you loved me
I just knew
I just knew
So you were there
You loved me
And you didn't want me to leave
Because I was at your parents' house
Your sister was there
So you were there
And I was walking out the door
Your parent's door
And you said
Come back in the morning Wel have breakfast
And I knew from that
That I'd won
That you loved me
But then I woke up
So I don't know what we ate
Or if we ran off together
And raised cats
like crazy people

Or fought at bed bath and beyond over comforter sets
That would make me happy too
Because
You were there

After awhile
He stares at her chair
That she no longer sits in
Slowly sipping his coffee
Seated in his brown leather jacket
It was the last thing she bought him
He wears it beyond acceptability
And gets nervous when he thinks of hanging it up
He talks to her
Even though she's gone
And the wheel of life's fortune has taken her in another direction
He slowly washes his cup with the dish rag
She got from the dollar store
It has chickens on it
And she always loved chickens
Like a haunted house
His empty heart
And empty home
Are ruled by the ghost of their love
Dancers in an ugly world
Who danced together
Making lite of the hell of human existence
Making love like death was at their door
Compulsive love
The kind that hits the veins of a lonely heart
And refuses to let go
He retires to the living room and reads the newspaper
He will fall asleep
And dream of her gigantic smile and cotton dresses
And tiny hands

Soon
Very soon
After Awhile

Once more with feeling

Many times the thing that we desperately want

We really don't need

And the thing we think we can't live without

Would kill us if we caught it

I stare in the mirror

Pinching extra skin

And weighing my soul

The first chapter of my life was heavy

Like a storm that has no mercy ripping thru a farmers field

This next chapter finds me wrinkled

And nervous to hope

Or believe

In anything

I wade in a quiet acceptance

That the most important love I should seek is my own

After the house fire of my past

I mine the debris for pieces of me that still work

And are useful

Accepting that the only light I need

Is my own

Glasses

My eyesight is perfect

My heart sight not so much

Seeing you with him

Punched me in the face

I listen as the ice dances in the glasses of White Russians

As I swim in the thoughts that I'm short

Of being accepted

And tall on being not good enough

Lots of love songs

Are there any songs for those?

Afraid of love

Who refuse to try in the first place?

Because love looks great on paper

But always leads one to glasses

Either adjusting theirs or proclaiming

WTF

Or drinking steadily

From a flight of loneliness elixir

And stating under breath never again

Alcohol attacks the senses slowly

Love all at once

With Cupid's nasty arrow

Shakespeare wrote of love allot

I predict he drank of love just as much

I hope you're happy

He's very tall

And acceptable

Like the beer I just ordered

Daydreams
We are all
Playing piano in a dark dingy bar
Dreaming of Carnegie hall
Slipping into daydreams of a life we wish we had
A life we crave
Settling for a life that comes to us like a bad hand at the card table
And lovers who are less than love
Drinking from the fountain
Of what could be
If we'd only rebel

Into Darkness

The Wolves of War

Snarl at the door

Women and children first

That's who they go for

When it's more than just a war

Women and children first

A Vampire in love

I want to drink you

like my life depends on it

Devour you

In the worst way

The sounds of your moans and screams

My music to study by

Study you

As you are the only subject that matters

To me

I am death

Without you

The angel of my soul you are

And this demon bows his head

And admits

Unworthiness

And a desperate need and love for you

Take shelter in my coffin built for 2

Lay your head on this chest

That houses my heart

That beats solely for you

And only when you are near

Hells Basement

Looking up

Just to see hell

I've got a coffin

Built for two

For a love that never dies

Your red dress awaits you

For our Black wedding

My black heart is red for you

And I'll always be true blue

I'm not the boy next door

Just a lonely Vampire

Who loves you?

Revolver

Every Turn of the wheel of fortune

Is like playing Russian roulette

I don't know what the outcome will be

When I pull the trigger on my Gun of life choices

I know that I'm old

I know that I'm lonely

And that this dark world stinks

love feels like a cage

And I don't want it

It's not me

You see that man on top of the cake in a

Tuxedo who is smiling

Fuck him

I'm not that

I'm a beast

I drink and howl at the moon

And rage against life's unfairness

And love feels like a cage

I feel trapped

And cornered

And I'm gonna run

I'm gonna set fire to this ship

Cause love feels like a cage

Lucifer

I must confess to you my darkest secret

I don't belong here

Or anywhere

Or in any group

And love is just not for me

I try so hard to fit in or belong to someone

Or somewhere and I am always found out

To be lacking in something that

Well makes me okay

Or acceptable

And I just don't have that

My parents left me at 11

And I've never been right since

My wings are dirty and torn

From Years of wanting to fly

But never just quite making it

Off the ground

I can fake it for a minute or two

But much longer just won't do

So I sit here at this bar

Alone

Watching lovers love

Under the artificial lights

And smell the stale beer and the incense of squashed dreams and hopes

I embrace a heaven

That only exits in my mind

Pieced together

From memories and foolish hope

15 Minutes

We're all on Candid camera now

A world of lonely and desperate people

Doing therapy on Tik Tok

Shaking whatever ass or heart we have

In front of the camera so that someone will see

And respond

Our message in a bottle is a video

Isolated in our rooms and lives

We reach out the only way we know how

And beg to be loved and accepted

If only for 15 minutes

Here we mourn

At the park

Walking Our laps

Or sitting on benches made of wood

She eats the past like Chocolate

Drowning in its Debt

Swimming in the darkness of her life with eyes closed

No light to be felt or seen

Breaking up with God

Because he's never called back

Or answered her anyway

She will worship herself

Instead

And pray at the altar of Self love

Tossing her Rosary into the pond

And watching it slowly fade away into the waters depths

Like her faith

Various and Sundry

I sit and take communion with my White Russian

As I remember feasting on your flesh

All I have left of you are

Memories

They are my opium

And I am an addict

I starve without you

I am your disciple

lost in the desert of your rejection

Taste you again is all I want

Hear the sermons of your lectures

The psalms of your voice

The gaze of your eyes as I get baptized in them

And find the God I've always wanted

Perfekt

I miss you

I keep the photo of us at the beach

It's the last proof that I am human

Or once was

I miss your face

I regret not touching it more

I regret not loving you better

I miss your Voice

It's like my favorite song

I'm sorry it didn't work out

Or what once maybe was couldn't be fixed

Again

Like a historic building

That's burned to the ground

And will only exist in the memories of those

Who cared or treasured it

Monday School

Breathing Underwater

Clutching my crucifix

I have no one to blame but myself for my life

I let my scape goat free

And took the blame

I sit here in my prison

And I wait for you to set me free

Preachers talk of heaven

They say clouds and harps

And an eternity with your loved ones

I don't know about that

But I do know I just want to wake up next to you

Drink coffee

And grow fat

Together like beef cattle about to be sold

And nightly talks in the bathroom as we brush our teeth

To jump into slumber

So that we can do our 9 to 5

And pay the bills

The next day

And steal moments of humanity in between

The music of the crickets is our wedding song

As anything louder just wouldn't do

Dopamine

Many run from pain

The poet marries it

Makes love to it

Like a cheap hooker in a back alley

With no lights and lots of fumbling for release

When pain appears

The poet goes hello old friend

My constant companion

The poet does not shriek or run

He grabs his quill

And turns his pain

Into a human cry

A cry for love

A cry for acceptance

A cry for truth about life and its ugliness

Which makes humans of us all

Warlock

In my garden I slither

Up a tree of memories

That I hope to create with you

The only light that exists in my dark soul

Is you

I am a dark and solitary thing

An outcast

An exile

If magick were in my hands

I'd give it all to you

I'd make flower petals fall at your feet

As you walk

And the sun would always be in your favor

Rain would never touch you

And clouds would form your face

My favorite face

I ride a broom

Thru the thick of the night

To the darkest woods that mirror my soul

And in the distance I see the sun start to rise

And caress the grass and the trees

Like the holiest of devoted lovers

And I think of you

The sun to my moon

We share the same universe

But dance always apart

Dive into your flames

My soul's desire

You are the light

And I am the dark

Breakfast and then a funeral

The alarm clock by my bed is loud

But the one in my heart is ever so silent

Like the scream of one who has not met their quota of living a fulfilled life

Run

Run like you are on fire

And the waters of experience are the only thing that can put you out

Live

Live like there's no dinner today

Only lunch

And lunch becomes a gourmet meal

Kiss

Kiss as if your breathing depends on it

And it does

And the lips you kiss will be your last

Don't go to the grave

Without having climbed

A mountain of experiences

That takes one's breath away

Long before death

Chooses too

Stay, don't go

You feel that you're at the end of your rope
And life won't get any better
Stay, don't go
You're drowning in darkness and you think that's all you'll ever know
Stay, don't go
You've made mistakes
And failed at things
Stay don't go
You don't see a tomorrow
Because of the darkness of today
Stay, don't go
You feel all alone
And like no one cares
Stay don't go
Don't listen to those awful voices in your head
None of its true
Stay, don't go
Just reach out
Pick up that phone
Tomorrow is a new day
Please I beg you
Stay, don't go

Electric witchcraft

Our eyes met
And we studied each other
Like two wild animals who found what they want to devour
In this jungle called life
The dance of soulmates who secretly rejoice
Because their other half has finally stopped fucking around and shown
themselves
I confidently introduced myself
You acted like it was an everyday thing
Our meeting
Women are such horrible liars
Both of us holding our brooms
We know we aren't like anyone else
Our pointed hats are a dead give away
The power between us was as noticeable as an atom bomb at a scrabble
game factory
With letters everywhere floating in the air
And words beyond the ability to be formed
We tried to shake hands but shocked each other
And then both laughed
Hoping we could ground ourselves in this true love

Drink till you come home

The irony is not lost on me
As I sit at the bar
Dwight yoakam is singing about a love that was lost not won
I carry your crumpled picture in my pocket
Bordering on pathetic
Is my middle name
It isn't until the second glass
That the memories of you start to flow
And my head hangs lower
Than the mistakes I've made losing you
Men are funny
That's a nice way of putting it
We want to be close
But we also want to be free
Funny is a nice way of saying stupid
And this cowboy is quite stupid

Our dystopia

This is the meanest we've ever been
So full of hate
And rage
We plant our flags
And we kill our brother
Our sister
Our friend
If their flag doesn't look like ours
We suckle at the teet of social media
And cry for human connection
But we've forgotten what that is or was
We know we need love
But we're just so full of hate
Where does this go
What will we become?
It's not good
I can tell you
Like Jorel warning Krypton
We are past the danger zone
We must turn back
Before it's too late
Our children are watching
Our children are watching

The Repentance of Don Juan

I am tired

Tired of kissing lips that kiss me back only once

Tired of staring into the eyes of heaven and watching them walk away

Tired of joining hands with love only to have it let go

Tired of lying and being lied to

Tired of faking sainthood to win the heart of an angel with even faker wings

My heart seeks the destiny of Byron's Misfit hero

I want to reach put my hand, the extension of my tired heart and find a warm cheek to grace in the ghostly darkness

Having the author of my life's story so write it that the cheek I find will be the one I union with forevermore.

Crawl

Crawl out from beneath you
The weight of your hate
Took my everything
Stop being fake
Own the truth
It's ok
To be angry
When it's about being abused
Dig
Dig
Dig
Down deep to that person that you lost
Take off that mask
And heal
Heal
By being everything you have always wanted to be
Stare liars and lies in the eyes
And yell with all of your soul
No more

Henry Rollins Karaoke

Don't fit
Never did
Lucky you
I guess
You're lucky
You belong
Belong
To what
To whom
To why
Can you
Think
Think for
Yourself
Be an alien
Right up front
Are you
Mad
Are you sad?
Can you say it out loud?
Can you stand against the masses?
Tell them to kiss your
Are you tough?
Are you rough?
Will you fold and sell out
Just to belong
Hey punk I'm talking to you
Hey punk can you be true

Sleep like a baby

I sleep like a baby

Who is hungry

Who is scared

Who doesn't know what's going on in the world

I sleep like a baby

Who is alone

And wants

And needs

Someone

Someone

To call its home

I sleep like a baby

Whose needs aren't being met

Who cries

And cries

And cries

Hoping

Hoping to cry no more

Crappily Never After

I guess you're not coming
At least not my way
I guess you're not coming
What can I say?
No Majorettes for me
Someone else is the lucky guy I guess
I'm sorry I didn't impress
Or wasn't good enough
Fuck
I own that position
I've tried hard all of my life
You're just another mountain
I couldn't climb
I'm not just saying that because you're taller than me
But read it like you will
I hope I never see you again
Or hear you've married some awesome guy
Not to be a shitty poet
That will fucking make me cry

Old Punk

Fuck your 9 to 5
Fuck your just staying alive
Fuck your missiles and your hate
Fuck your taxes
And your rape
I'm an old punk in Converse shoes
I scream out loud
I don't sing the fucking blues
I'm an old punk
I don't fit in any way
Piss on your class system
And your politics
They aren't for me
They are yours all yours
I just want to fucking Breathe
I just want to live and be free to have what everyone else has
Sick of your walls
And obstacle
Shove your credit cards up your ass
I ain't got class and never did
Just my heart
And it's still a kid

Hair

I want to play with your hair in the worst way
Do whatever it takes to make you smile
And see me with those eyes of yours as someone you want next to you
In the real life game of thrones
There are no dragons and a real queen isn't to be found
Unless they've found you
I'm sorry about that jester you were with
He didn't make you laugh
He didn't see how amazing you are
Smart
Beautiful
And how your voice can command the sun
I am a total peasant but I'll be whatever it takes to steal your gaze
Give me a sword and I'll fight
A jester's tunic
I'll dance and fall to make you laugh
I'll be your mirror when days are shit
And you forget how badass you are
I'll never be king
And that I've accepted
But I'd love for you to be my Queen

Ring Finger

He Places his hand palm down over the cup of coffee

A silent way to say that he has had enough to the waitress

He has swiped right for years

The messages received are never serious

And the conversation never long

Or really going anywhere

Love is not possible anymore he thinks

At least not for him

Not that any of his all thumbs attempts were love anyway

He knew a man who lost his leg

Once

But could still feel it

Occasionally he would play with his ring finger

As if a ring were still there

Never again he thought

Never again

The sword that fell to earth

He lay motionless in the field
His only company the empty whiskey bottles who lay next to him
His jeans wreaked in piss
And his mouth had vomit stains from the night before
He stood up slowly
Like he was fighting for his life against gravity
Wiping the goop from his eyes
He was suddenly frightened by the large Spectre
Before him
In the middle of the farmers field
And very out of place
A large sword was stuck in the ground
Its metallic silver was gold like a gun
And its rich black wrapped handle
Called to him
Like a drunken lover
He studied it as he had only seen swords in movies
His life up to this point has been less than glorious
He was the town outcast
The town drunk
Who no one liked
He couldn't keep a job and was that one person who everyone talked
about when they wanted to feel superior or give young people a warning
about wasting their lives
His right shoulder still ached from when he tried to be something or
someone in high school and played football freshman year
It did not take
And he did not last half a season
Nervously he grasped the swords handle slowly like grabbing a rattlesnake

And as he did he felt something shift
Shift within the very hidden fibers of his being
Rage
All of the rage he'd been drowning with alcohol and self-belittlement
Just rushed to the surface as he lifted the sword in the air and felt a new
strength flow thru his veins that he'd never felt before
His eyes blackened
Like onyx
And his muscles instantly became toned and visible
He had only one thing on his mind
And that was the punishment of all who had wronged him
It was dawn and he made his way to the mouth of the town
Just as everyone was beginning to head out and start their day
No one really had ever paid attention to him
That would change
The diner was packed with people fueling up and the town sheriff was
inside eating his morning dose of eggs and bacon
"What the fuck is Fred doing" exclaimed a patron
"Is that, is that a goddamn sword"?
Fred our antagonist's name
Lifted his sword with both hands and crashed it down in the middle of the
sheriffs car
Easily severing it in half like a sandwich
He turned toward the diner and slashed his way into the building
The sheriff fired his entire gun at him but the bullets seemed to meet the
swords blade no matter what part of Fred he fired at
Until eventually he was empty and the diner floor was covered in severed
body parts including the sheriffs
Fred made his way out into the street and one by one has unsuspecting
townsfolks drove by he cleaved their car into almost effortlessly

The other two sheriff cars came at him as he made his way thru the town
unleashing his rage and hatred for decades of not belonging
And enjoying his new found power
The two sheriffs cornered him into an alley and began firing shots which
the sword deflected almost effortlessly
Until Fred was tearing apart their squad cars and eventually them like a
moving blender

Like a lone gunslinger Fred slowly walked down the once peaceful town's
street covered in blood and stopping to study the piles of body parts
And car wreckage that lay in his previous path
He grinned now feeling a strange power he never had known before
If he keeps walking he will be in a couple of miles into the next town
That was a thought that he relished
He wondered to himself
How far could he go?
Could he literally just take over the world and be its king
As he turned to accept his path heading to the next town he saw the sky
open and a large cylindrical craft appear as if out of no where
The Craft was hovering facing him as if in some kind of stand off
Who is this he thought
Maybe it's the owner of the sword
Maybe they want it back
He gripped the sword even tighter and knew that if he ever lost it
He would just be that weak loser he once was
Powerless and afraid
And he could never go back to being that

Outside

Everywhere I go

Workers are exhausted

And their numbers are fewer

But the malls and stores are full

I see people walking that tightrope of losing their shit and faking it's ok

What is going on?

War over seas

And war right here

Everyone is in their tribe

And all bets are off

Madmen are popping up like flies

Is anyone safe?

Grandpa is driving America into a ditch

Should he even be driving at his age?

Where is everyone?

People are dying

People are crying

People are lying

Saying this won't change the way things have been

I swiped my credit card today

Buy now pay later

Feel the opium hit my veins

As I find happiness like a good little mouse who does what the commercials

say to do

Consume

Buy

The rich hate the poor because they can't play

The game that they made

Feel the earth begin to quake

That's a million cash registers
Shaking from stress
They don't want to be money machines anymore
Paul was right
We love khakis
We love Kardashians
We aren't happy till we are rich in stuff
And poor in love
All of this is collapsing
Like a bridge with too much weight

From the nasty world outside

I wish I was your hero
The man you looked up to
And thought about
When you wake up
And when you go to bed
I wish I was your hero
like the guy on those smutty romance novel covers
You know
The pirate
The vampire
The vagabond you turn heroic with your love
Who saves the day
I do not fly
I don't wear spandex
Trust me you don't want that
But I love you very much
And always have
And like the loyalist dog
I'll never leave
And your company is all I want
And when the world is dark and scary
I will be your home
Your safe place
To run to
to hide
From the nasty world outside

Face

She touched his face lovingly

But was filled with rage at him

For the love he had awakened in her

Love is scary and dangerous and never works out and almost always leads

to one's own destruction

Playing with it

The idea that it's okay

And that this time won't be like the last time

Is a song she never wanted to hear from the record player in her heart

Trying to communicate with her head

Rage it is

And tears

And fears

For that all too human desire

To hold the hand of lasting love

The hand that holds you back

And props you up and opens the door and packs your lunch

And smacks your ass

And waves goodbye as you head to work

And grabs you tightly as you come home

From the nasty world outside

Horoscope

Damn these stars and planets
I don't want anyone
Anything
Or any power other than myself to determine my fate
Fixed
It's fixed my lot in this life
How it will go
How it will be for me
By what
When I was born
Or the lines on the palm of my hand
Or if I was the seventh son
Of the seventh son
Who was born on Tuesday
During a leap year
Really my fate is fixed
By who
Jupiter
Or some God
On mount Olympus
No thanks
I lace up my punk rock sneakers
And declare anarchy
I'm rebelling
My past has been dark
But I'm in charge now
And I'm taking it all back
My today

And my tomorrow will be mine
Because I said it will be
I don't need fairies luck
Or Mars to care
I care
For me for myself
And I will be the author of my now and more
From this day forth

(Written for Wall Street News Agency June 6th 2022)

Hell is for Women and Children of War

Behind The Docuseries Into Darkness

With Journalist David Thomas and Vincent Lyn of the International Human Rights Commission and The Social Council of the United Nations

By David Thomas of

This is News with David Thomas

My name is David Thomas I am a Citizen journalist in America who uses Journalism as a form of activism in America and in my community as well as globally to connect and educate people to the issues that we encounter in our world. I have frequently Interviewed Mr. Lyn who I ironically met over a decade ago when I was losing a Jiu-jitsu match at a Martial Arts Tournament in Ohio.

We filmed 6 Interviews over the course of Mr. Lyn's Humanitarian Mission to the Ukraine. The origin of the idea to film a docuseries of his mission began on March 15th 2022 when I interviewed Mr. Lyn about his recent Mission to Syria and our Interview Not only focused on the Syrian Civil war and the Plight of Syrian Orphans amid the unrest and devastation in the Middle east, but also touched on what Putin's game plan could possibly be to want to invade the Ukraine as well as would the United Nations actually intervene and do more than talk.

Each episode of our docuseries became increasingly hard to film as stories of war Crimes and the devastating effects of the war on Ukraine's Women and children were unearthed. Strategic Bombings of Train stations filled with Civilians as well as towns who had been occupied by Russian soldiers and the murders and Rapes of innocent Civilians.

To be quite honest half way thru the Docuseries I wanted to stop, but pressed on as I felt that the stories of what is happening to innocent Ukrainian Woman and Children must be told.

From our Interviews I learned that Russia's war Plans are to focus on what I call "Historical and Generational Intimidation" That Is they hope to leave a mark culturally in the Ukraine by focusing on the Rape, abuse and torture of Women and Children as well as Civilians, so that generations of Ukrainians will be talking about and fearful of the Russians.

Many things are taking place right now the good is that neighboring countries like Latvia are taking in Ukrainian Refugees, Women and Children, and helping them to get homes and jobs and new Lives. The horrible of it is that Human traffickers are also targeting Refugees who are escaping and Kidnapping them to be used in Human Sex Trafficking in Europe.

The most difficult interview with Mr. Lyn was when he described a bus of children he encountered who had all of their teeth Knocked out by Russian Soldiers and who also had been Raped. It was by then that I knew that this was more than just War for Putin.

Our Docuseries with the help of an Amazing editor from Mount Union College Named Josh Evans helped us to create a fleshed out Documentary that is around 10 minutes in length that I called " Into Darkness, an in depth look at Russia's war Crimes against The Women and Children of the Ukraine."

The Only Light in Into Darkness is the part where Vincent Lyn and his team are actually able to rescue and help some refugees escape. One refugee was a woman with two small children, who if it were not for the efforts of Lyn's humanitarian Mission could've quite possibly become another victim to the wolves of Human Trafficking.

At the end of this docuseries we post a picture of that woman her two children and Mr. Lyn and to this day that picture haunts me.

It is a painful reminder of who suffers the Brunt of war the most, and that is the Earths Children.

Mr. Lyn's Humanitarian mission was to deliver food and supplies to the Ukrainian's, help refugees escape and create dialogue with neighboring countries diplomats and leaders to support this exodus and to report to the United Nations and the Human Rights Commission what he saw firsthand and learned from the Ukrainian people.

Mr. Lyn and a team will be going back to the Ukraine in July on a second Humanitarian Mission.

Made in the USA
Coppell, TX
21 June 2022

79056307R00067